The Curious Little Kitten

Story By Bernadine Cook
Pictures By Remy Charlip

Young Scott Books, N.Y.

Once upon a time there was a turtle.
He wasn't a big turtle,
nor a middle-sized turtle,
but just a little turtle.
And he lived in a small garden
that had a little pool in it.

U. S. 950153

In the house next door there was a kitten.
Not a big kitten, nor a middle-sized kitten,
but just a little kitten.
And he was a very curious little kitten at that.

Every day the little turtle
would walk around in the garden.
Now, turtles cannot go very fast
because their legs are so short. So they go slowly.
So, the little turtle walked around the garden
slowly, very slowly.

He would stop,
lift up his head,
and then he would go again.

One day he was walking around like this,

when the curious little kitten
ventured into the garden.

Now, the little kitten
had never seen a turtle before,
because he was just a little kitten
and he hadn't been around very much.
He was surprised.
He stopped and looked at the turtle.

Then he came a little closer,
and a little closer.
But he was very careful,
because he wasn't just quite sure
what this funny-looking creature was.
When he was very close to the little turtle…

the turtle stopped.

And the kitten stopped.
The turtle looked at the kitten.
And the kitten looked at the turtle.
Then . . .

the kitten took one little paw
and slapped at the turtle with it.

The kitten's eyes nearly popped right out!
Because—do you know what happened?

The little turtle's head disappeared!
Just like that!
He pulled it right inside
his little turtle shell!

Well!
The little kitten took a step backwards.
And then he sat down.

Pretty soon he got up,
and walked around the little turtle,
very slowly and very carefully.
He looked at this funny creature
that could make his head disappear.

Maybe, he thought,
if I slap at him again,
his head might come out.

So he slapped him again.
The little kitten's eyes
nearly popped out a second time!

Because—do you know what happened?

The little turtle's legs disappeared!
He pulled them right inside
his little turtle shell.
Well!

He stood and looked at this funny creature
that could make his head and his legs disappear.

He didn't know quite what to think.
So he just stood right there,
looking at the little turtle.

And the little turtle sat right there
inside his little turtle shell.

Pretty soon the little turtle
began to let his legs down out of his shell again,
very slowly.

The little kitten took a step backwards.

Then the little turtle poked his little nose
out of his little turtle shell.

And the little kitten
took another step backwards.

Then the little turtle poked his whole head
out of his little turtle shell.

and the little kitten took another step
backwards.

And the little turtle took a step toward the kitten.
And the kitten took another step backwards.
And the turtle took a step.
And the kitten took a step.
Then the turtle stopped.
And the kitten stopped.

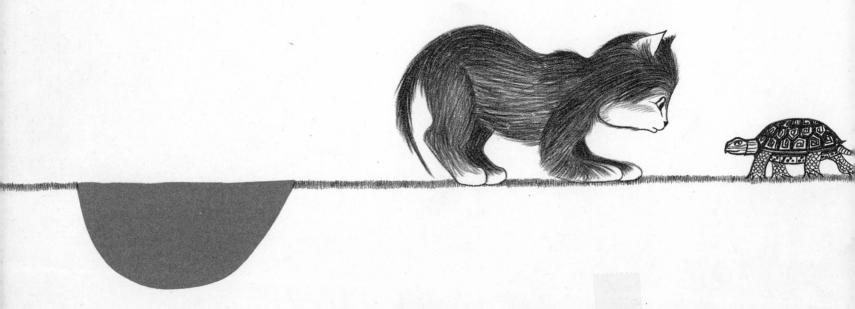

Now, the kitten was walking backwards.
He didn't see the pool of water,
not very far behind him.
But it was there.

Pretty soon the little turtle
took another,
and another,
and another step.

And the little kitten backed up
another,
and another,
and another step.
Until the pool was right exactly behind him.

U. S. 950153

The turtle stopped.
And the kitten stopped.
The turtle looked.
And the kitten looked.
Then the turtle took one more step.
And the kitten took one more step.

And, oh, my!

The kitten fell,
SPLASH!
backwards,
right into the pool of water.

Now, kittens don't like water much,
except to drink
sometimes.
So . . .

the kitten jumped out of the water,
and ran past the turtle just as fast
as his little kitten legs could carry him

right back to the house next door,
where he belonged.

But the turtle kept right on going,
and slid down into the water,
because turtles just love water.

After that, the little kitten
didn't go into the garden any more.
He would just come as far as the fence
and look through it at the little turtle.
But he didn't go into that garden again.
And he never walked backwards any more.
Oh, no!

Because little kittens just don't like water!